Brave Dog
Bonnie

BEL MOONEY

Illustrated by Sarah McMenemy

**WALKER
BOOKS**

First published 2009 by Walker Books Ltd
87 Vauxhall Walk, London SE11 5HJ

This edition published 2013

2 4 6 8 10 9 7 5 3 1

Text © 2009 Bel Mooney
Illustrations © 2009 Sarah McMenemy

The right of Bel Mooney and Sarah McMenemy to be identified as
author and illustrator respectively of this work has been asserted by
them in accordance with the Copyright, Designs and Patents Act 1988

This book has been typeset in StempelSchneidler

Printed and bound in Great Britain by Clays Ltd, St Ives plc.

British Library Cataloguing in Publication Data:
a catalogue record for this book is available from the British Library

ISBN 978-1-4063-5117-0

www.walker.co.uk

For Daisy Dimbleby
B.M.

For my godson, George
S.M.

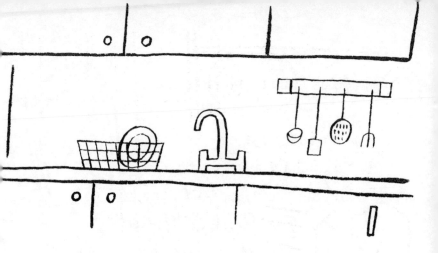

Scaredy-Pup

"You'll like London – it's cool!" said Zack as he held a dog choc up high, trying to make Bonnie dance on her hind legs.

But Princess Daisy the (annoying) chihuahua was racing round the room, so Bonnie needed to keep her dignity. She sat tight by Harry's trainers.

"Lovely shops in London!" said Susie.

"Who wants shops?"

Harry loved hanging out with his friends. But that morning he'd had news that was good and bad at the same time, and now he wasn't really in the mood for talking.

"You'll have a great time with your dad, Haz," said Zena.

"But…" Harry began. He picked Bonnie up and snuggled his face into her silky white ears. That always made him feel better. In his mind he could see his mum's cross face as she told him that his father had invited him to London for some of half-term – and what was he thinking?

"But, Mum, I'd like to see his new place," Harry said.

"Yes, and that's not all that's new!" Mum snapped.

So nothing was decided yet.

"The thing is…" Harry stopped again.

"Go on, Harry," encouraged Susie.

"Well, my dad … he's got this girlfriend, and she lives with him, and so that means I have to meet her…"

"Oh. Scary," nodded Zack.

"I'm sure she'll be really sweet," said Zena.

"Yeah, *right*," Harry grunted.

"Yeip, yeip," squeaked Princess Daisy, making a little run at Bonnie.

The Maltese knew she had to show the chihuahua whose patch this was, so she chased her round and round until the smaller dog lay down to say "You win!"

When they'd all stopped laughing, Susie scooped Princess Daisy up and Zena returned to the subject worrying Harry.

"So what are you going to do?"

Harry sighed. "Mum says I can't go, but I've *got* to or Dad'll be hurt; and yet I don't really want to, so…"

"I've got an idea!" said Susie.

"What?"

"Take Bonnie with you. Won't she make you feel braver?"

Harry looked at Susie. He opened his mouth to protest that he didn't need to feel *brave* because he didn't feel *scared*—

"What?" roared Zack. "The scaredy-pup who shivers when she's having a bath?"

And that was the end of that conversation as they all dissolved into giggles.

🐾   🐾   🐾

Later Harry heard Mum on the phone to Dad. She spoke in that cool voice he knew so well. It always used to drive his dad mad.

"Look, David, it's impossible. If you can't come to get him, I'm not sending him on the train by himself. No, I'm not being unhelpful…"

"Can I speak to Dad?" asked Harry.

His mother frowned and handed him the phone.

"Hi, Dad."

"Hi, big guy, how's it going?"

"Fine."

"Good. We're working out how to get you up to the big city. Car problems, you see. I can run you back down, but I can't collect you."

"Hey, Dad? Would it be OK if I brought Bonnie?"

"The scary miniature mutt? Why not? If she misbehaves we'll have her made into a pair of gloves for Kim. Now, put your mother back on."

Harry picked
Bonnie up and left
the room so he wouldn't have to hear his
mother's voice any more. Minutes later
she came and sat next to him on the sofa,
zapping the TV off.

"You wouldn't really take Bonnie and
leave me here all on my own, would you,
love?"

That's how it is with grown-ups, Harry
thought. Whatever you do, they turn it

round so that somehow they're sad – and it's all your fault.

An angry voice in his head snarled, *I didn't want Dad to leave, and I didn't want to move here and have to start a new school, and I didn't even want a silly little girly lapdog from the dogs' home!*

But as soon as he'd had that thought, Bonnie stretched out a paw and touched his hand, looking reproachfully up at him with those coal-black eyes as if she knew what was in his mind.

Feeling guilty, Harry bent down to plonk a kiss on her head. "Aw, I suppose not, Mum," he said miserably.

But help was on its way. Mum's friend Olga turned up at the door, and soon knew the whole story. Sometimes Harry thought Olga was like the nicest sort of good witch, with her wild hair, crazy coloured clothes and her way of solving problems.

"…so you see, it's impossible for him to go – and I hope *you* understand that, Harry, my pet," his mum finished.

Olga stared straight into her eyes. "It's not actually *impossible*, Ann," she said.

Mum frowned. "What do you mean?"

"It could be very easy – if you want it to be. There's a new exhibition  at the National Gallery I've been meaning to go and see. It's about time I had a day in London. So Harry can travel up on the train with me."

Harry stared at his mum, hardly daring to breathe. Until that moment, he hadn't realized how much he *did* want to go and see Dad's flat.

To go and see Dad. Even if it did mean meeting his new partner.

Bonnie was looking at Harry intently. As always, he felt the little dog could read his mind. It was as if she could hear all those awful shouting matches before Dad had packed a suitcase and left; as if she could see how much Harry hated leaving where they'd lived before, and could taste the salty tears he'd tried to hide from his mum. As if she could smell his fear as he'd started a new school, and could feel how his fingers used to curl round the velvety ears of his big imaginary dog Prince for comfort. As if she *knew* all about those difficult days.

Sometimes Harry suspected that even though she was so small, Bonnie still knew more than they did. Things didn't have to be spoken aloud for dogs to understand.

"…so you see, Ann? It's easy," Olga chattered on. "And we'll get *you* organized with lots of lovely things to do that weekend so you won't miss Harry too much."

"And Bonnie," Harry added.

"Must you take her?" asked Mum. "Won't she be frightened by all the noise, all the traffic…?"

"Please, Mum," he begged.

"Every dog should see London once," said Olga with a smile. "After all, it's their capital city too!"

And so it was decided.

🐾　🐾　🐾

"You'll have to make sure Bonnie's always wearing her collar – just in case she gets lost," said Zena when Harry went next door to tell them the news.

"How could she get lost with me taking care of her?" laughed Harry.

Just then the twins' mum
swept into the sitting-
room, bracelets
jangling. "Guess
what, Harry?" she said.
"We've decided to have a
big supper party that Saturday
night you're in London and ask
lots of old pals we haven't seen
for years – and get your mum
along too. We'll make sure she
has a fab time. Take care of her
for you. Good idea, hey?"

Harry bent down to scoop Bonnie
up, and pretended to wrestle with her
on his knee. He needed to hide his face.
Mrs Wilson knew he was worried about
leaving his mum, and what she'd just said
made his eyes prickle.

Suddenly Bonnie jumped down and tore
around the room. She grabbed hold of the

edge of
one of their
colourful rugs
and started to tug
at it, growling.

"Stop that, Bons!" shouted
Harry, glad of the distraction.

Mrs Wilson laughed, even though the rug
was rather smart. Harry liked that she didn't
fuss much about things.

"Let's hope she doesn't wreck your dad's
new place," she said. "Are you looking
forward to seeing it?"

"Yeah, it'll be cool," said Harry, suddenly
wondering if there'd be a bedroom for him.

There was a silence, which Zack broke
by chanting, "Super-Wabbit, Super-Wabbit,
where have you been? I've been to London
to see the Queen!"

"Better watch it, Haz, or they'll make her
into a guardsman's hat," teased Zena.

"They'd have to catch her first!" laughed Harry, watching Zack try.

🐾   🐾   🐾

Two nights before his journey, Harry realized his mum had started to look a bit less down, and she even seemed quite excited about Saturday night with the Wilsons. They were eating chicken and jacket potatoes and peas at the kitchen table, and for once Mum didn't try to stop him slipping little pieces of chicken down to Bonnie.

"Are you looking forward to London, love?" she asked.

"Think so."

"Do you think you'll like Kim?"

"Who's Kim?" he asked, although he knew.

"You know perfectly well who she is, Harry! Dad's ... er ... friend."

19

"Oh, *her*. Probably not. Anyway, I expect she hates dogs."

Mum bent down and lifted Bonnie onto her knee. Then – to Harry's amazement – she dipped a finger into all the buttery-chickeny juices on her plate and let the dog lick it.

"Nobody could dislike Bons," she said softly.

There was a pause. Then Mum reached behind her for the brush and began to groom Bonnie's silky ears. "Better make you look pretty for London," she said. "I expect Kim is rather nice and pretty too."

Then Harry understood. His mum was *afraid*. That was what all this was about.

He jumped up and threw his arms
around her neck, so that Bonnie was nearly
squashed.

"No one's as nice or as pretty as you,
Mum. Nobody in the whole world!" he
yelled.

And Bonnie gave a loud "YIP!" in
agreement.

BONNIE perched on Harry's knee and looked out of the train window. What a rushing! Trees, fields, houses — all whizzing by, until she felt quite dizzy. She was trying to draw a doggy map in her head, so she could find her way back home, but it was all coming at her too quickly.

Whoosh! She didn't like the noise. It made her nervous. People walked past and pointed at her, and once a small boy leaned across and poked her hard. "Doggy-woggy! Ickle doggy-woggy!" he screamed.

His mum pulled him away. "Leave the dear little thing alone, darling!"

Thing? I'm not a thing. I'm a very big dog!

Olga was talking to Harry. Bonnie could tell
he was doing his best to answer nicely, but he
didn't want to.

Poor Harry! Bonnie could feel how nervous he
was, right through his arms, his hands, his fingers.
It was a mixture of wanting what was about
to happen – wanting it *so* much – and then not
wanting it at all. Wishing he were safe at home
with his mum instead.

Clatter, clatter, clatter went the train.

Is this me shaking, or is it this horrible noisy
monster? Bonnie wondered.

"Poor little scaredy-pup," whispered Harry
into her soft fur.

She felt him clutch her even more tightly as
the announcement came over the loudspeaker:
"Paddington Station is our next stop. Please make
sure you have all your belongings..."

He's trying to be brave, Bonnie thought. Because
there's no choice, really.

☆ LOST DOG ☆

"There they are!" said Harry, glimpsing two figures in the distance. He hoped Olga couldn't read the mixture of feelings on his face.

"I'm looking forward to meeting your dad," she whispered as they walked along the platform to the ticket barrier.

Bonnie pulled on her lead – and nearly tripped a man up. He turned round and scowled. Nobody seemed to look down at the little dog and smile, like they always did back home. Harry decided that London was unfriendly as well as scary. His heartbeats seemed to echo all around the vast arc of the station roof, so that he thought everyone must be able to hear them.

Ahead, Dad waved. Next to him stood a young woman with short black hair, wearing a bright purple jacket and a broad smile.

How do you *do* this? Harry asked himself. How *can* you be friendly to someone your mum doesn't like? But then Dad… Oh, help me, somebody! Why is it all so hard?

As if she had heard, Bonnie suddenly turned and jumped up at him, begging to be picked up, which gave him something to do.

Then Olga took over. "You must be Dave," she said, holding out her hand. "I'm Olga, Ann's friend."

"Good to meet you, and thanks for bringing this one up to town," replied

Harry's dad, in that extra-bright voice he
used when he felt a bit shy.

"These *two*!" laughed Olga, pointing to
Bonnie.

"Hello, mate!" said Dad, ruffling Harry's
hair. "And say hello to my friend Kim.
Kim, this is Harry. And dog!"

"She's not called Dog – she's Bonnie," said
Harry, making a great fuss over putting her
on the ground, so that nobody could see his
face grow red.

Kim squatted down and tried to pat Bonnie. "It's really lovely to meet you, Bonnie," she said. "I'm looking forward to getting to know you. And Harry too."

But Bonnie didn't like strangers. She shied away from Kim, spun in circles and then decided to attack Dad's jeans, snarling and growling and snapping. Then, when Harry pulled her away, she set up the fiercest yapping, right at Kim. Who drew back, looking upset.

"Oh, she doesn't like us, Dave," she said.

YAP YAP

"Sorry," mumbled Harry. She wasn't normally this noisy. Why was Bonnie behaving so badly? But at least it took the attention off *him*...

"She's very sweet when you get to know her," said Olga. "And now I think I'm going to leave you all. Not often I get a day out in London!"

Harry didn't want Olga to go. Suddenly she seemed like the one familiar thing in a frightening new world. He wished he were much smaller so he could catch hold of her hand and walk away. But instead he had to stay – with this person who was his dear old dad, yet felt like a stranger; and this even stranger woman by his side. Thank goodness he had Bonnie with him.

29

A small dog
can save your
life, Harry thought.
But it was Bonnie's life that needed saving
when the Tube train roared into the station
and they all crowded on. She'd never heard
such a clanking and rattling and clattering as
the train rushed through the black tunnels
– and she hated it with every white hair
on her body. Harry held her tight, but her

quivering and
shaking seemed
to go right through him.

It was only five stops to their destination. When they came out of the station, Harry found himself on a noisy street, where four buses rumbled by at once, and people yelled to each other across the road, and reggae music blasted out from a record shop with **DUB VENDOR** painted across it in big splashy lettering. He didn't know what that meant. He didn't know what *any* of this meant. He clung onto Bonnie for dear life.

"Hey, Harry, what's the mutt got at four corners of her body?" laughed Dad.

"What?"

"Her *legs*, big guy! Let her walk!"

So Bonnie's small, clean paws touched the long, dirty London pavement for the first time, and she sniffed a hundred scents which told her strange stories of men and dogs who had passed that way.

Dad's flat was the ground floor, with a small garden out the back. The patio door had a cat flap and Dad joked that it was a good job Bonnie came cat-sized, because she could let herself out whenever she needed to. Proudly he showed Harry the new kitchen, the sitting room with a huge TV and big squashy sofas, and two bedrooms, one large, one tiny. The smaller one contained a desk as well as a sofa bed, and by the computer Harry noticed a framed picture of him as a toddler, sitting on his dad's shoulders. They were both laughing at the camera, which must have been held by Mum. Seeing the photograph made him happy and sad at the same time.

"You grew up, mister," whispered Dad in his ear.

"Yeah," said Harry, thinking, *More than you know, Dad*.

🐾   🐾   🐾

By the time Harry had inspected the TV (a smart flat screen, not like the huge old set he and Mum had) and everything else in the flat, he was hungry. But when Kim offered him a piece of cake, he shook his head.

"What about Bonnie?" she asked. "I bought her some food. And her own bowl."

She showed him a tin of Bonnie's favourite food and a smart chrome bowl. Harry looked at her in astonishment.

"Did I guess right?" she asked.

He shrugged. "There's really only one brand."

"Well, I hope she's hungry, even if you're not."

"She never has much of an appetite in strange places," he replied in a flat voice. He hated himself. Kim was being so nice, yet he couldn't be nice back.

But Bonnie had spotted the dog food and wagged her tail. She sat with her pink tongue out, staring at Kim, who laughed. When she kneeled down Bonnie licked her hand.

"Look, Harry," she said. "Your lovely little dog's telling me I've done OK!"

"Good mutt!" called Dad from the sitting room.

They spent the rest of the day doing nothing much at all, because Harry's dad said he must be tired. Which was true. So they played some games, watched a DVD, ate Dad's best sausage and mash with onion gravy, then Kim showed Harry some of her drawings. She designed wallpaper, which Harry thought was a pretty weird sort of thing to do for a living. But he liked her drawing book, full of close-ups of flowers and leaves and birds, as well as sketches of boats and buildings.

"I like drawing," he said, despite himself.

"Well, when the weather's warmer maybe you and I can go sketching in the park," she suggested.

He shrugged. "Maybe."

He went into the study-cum-bedroom to call Mum on his mobile phone. Hearing her trying to be cheerful made him realize he had to go on being brave. It was the only way.

That night he curled up with Bonnie on
the sofa bed, listening to the sounds of the
city outside. Somebody shouted. A car alarm
went off. A group of girls ran past, shrieking
with laughter. And all the time buses and
cars – not to mention millions of distant
voices – hummed in the background, and he
even fancied he could feel the rumble of Tube
trains far beneath the surface of the city.

I'll never get to sleep here, he thought. But Bonnie snuggled up to him, and soon his eyes began to close.

🐾 🐾 🐾

They got up late the next day, and Dad announced it was time for brunch. "We're going to take you to our favourite place down the road," he said. "You can have the best fry-up in the world, Harry, and Kim loves the steak sandwich."

"What about Bonnie?" Harry asked.

"Oh, she'll stay here and be fine. They won't let her in the café."

Bonnie heard the dreaded word "stay" and knew she was about to be left behind. Her head drooped and her tail dragged on the ground. But there was no choice: Dad had planned the treat.

They closed the front door on the little dog and went to eat a brunch that was just as delicious as Dad had promised. Harry even started to like the buzz of the big city.

But a shock was waiting for him back at the flat. When Dad opened the front door, Harry waited for a white bundle to throw itself at him in relief that he had returned.

Nothing.

"Bonnie? Come, Bons! Come here, Mouse-Face!" he called.

Silence.

"The little scamp's hiding," said Dad.

"No, she's not," said Harry, running from room to room. "She wouldn't…"

"Bonnie!" called Kim.

There was no sign of the dog.

Kim unlocked the back door and they went out into the garden. One quick glance around showed that Bonnie wasn't there.

And then it was like a great big icy-cold hand was squeezing Harry's heart until all his breath was gone.

"Look!" he shouted, pointing to one corner.

There was a small hole in the fence. Beneath it something had scrabbled away at the soil, to make the escape route bigger.

Harry bent down and
picked some long white
hairs off the wood. He couldn't
speak. The three of them gazed at one
another in horror.

"She can't have gone far," reasoned Dad.
"We'll split up and walk round the block.
Harry, you come with me; Kim, you go the
other way."

There was panic in the air. They ran out
of the flat and started their search, looking
all about, calling her name, always believing

that round the next corner, or in some shop doorway, they would find the little white dog, her tongue lolling out with pleasure at seeing them.

Over an hour passed. They looked and looked. Kim went home to ring the police and the dog wardens, while Dad asked in every single shop in the area. Which was a lot. But nobody had seen the little white dog.

By now Harry was fighting back tears. When he and Dad joined Kim in the flat and she told them her phone calls had brought no joy, he finally gave in. "I – I w-w-w-wish we'd never come to L-L-London!" he sobbed.

Dad looked miserable. Kim put her arm round Harry and held him close. When the phone rang they all jumped. Harry's dad grabbed it.

Even from a few metres away Harry could hear his mum's voice. "WHAT ON EARTH'S HAPPENED, DAVE?" she yelled. "WHAT HAVE YOU DONE WITH MY DOG?"

"But how do you…?" he mumbled.

"I just came home to find a message on the answerphone. I couldn't believe it – then I realized that our number here is on Bonnie's collar. Oh, Dave, it was this *man*…"

Harry heard her start to cry, and he began to shiver, just like Bonnie on the Tube.

"For heaven's sake, Ann, what did he *say*?" asked his dad.

"He sounded horrible – rough, you know? Like a criminal. And he just said, 'We've got your dog,' and left a number. Oh, Dave, Bonnie's been *kidnapped*."

BONNIE didn't like being left behind. It's wasn't so bad at home, but this was a strange kennel and she didn't think Harry should treat her this way. How was she supposed to look after him when she was stuck here?

She jumped through the cat flap and started to explore. It took her a minute to sniff her way to the hole in the fence, another two minutes to make it bigger – and then she was out, ready to follow Harry wherever he'd gone.

The trouble was, the back of the flat led to an alleyway with smelly dustbins in it, and when Bonnie reached the street, it wasn't the one Harry had walked along just minutes earlier. When there was no scent of him she set off trying to find one, puffling along, head down – in the wrong direction.

Must find Harry, must find Harry, was all
she thought, not noticing anyone, not hearing
the buses and taxis braking as she crossed roads,
ignoring the children who pointed and cried,
"Oooh, look at that cute white dog all on its own!"
But suddenly she was penned in by feet and legs.
She heard gruff voices and laughter as she spun
round and round, trying to escape. She wriggled
madly as a very large pair of hands picked her up.

"Gotcha!"

She sank her tiny teeth into a fat finger and was
rewarded by a yell, then more laughter.

"Whoa — scary dog!" mocked a man's voice.
Arms pinned her so she could hardly breathe.
Where are they taking me? she thought.

And how will Harry
find me now?

Mean Mutt

"We have to keep calm," said Harry's dad as Kim and Harry stared at him, their faces pale.

"Will they ask for a ransom?" whispered Kim.

"I've got some pocket money," said Harry stoutly. His tears had gone. This was too frightening to cry about. He had to be brave for Bonnie – because, wherever she was now, the little dog was having to be even braver.

"The first thing I'm going to do is phone

that number they left," his dad said.

"But shouldn't we call the police?" asked Harry.

"No, not yet," said his dad grimly. "First, I'm going to have a word with this bloke, whoever he is."

"How could they steal Bonnie?" Harry burst out.

"She's a valuable-looking toy dog, love," said Kim quietly. "People pay good money for pets like her."

"Bonnie's worth more than money!" he said miserably.

Dad was reaching for the phone. He took a deep breath and dialled; Harry and Kim crowded next to him so they could hear. Kim had her arm round Harry's shoulders, but he didn't mind.

"Hello, mate," said Harry's dad when the call was answered.

"Who is this?" replied a man's voice.

Harry shivered. It didn't sound like a very nice voice. It was a rough, tough, gruff voice which he thought could easily turn very nasty indeed.

"My name's Dave. You left a message. About our dog."

Harry heard the man let out a sort of laugh – if you could call it a laugh. More like a bark, he thought.

"Oh – yeah, that's right."

"So?" said Dad, trying to sound as mean as possible. "What do you want?"

"What do we *want*?"

At that moment, they heard a distant, frantic yapping – as if Bonnie was in the next room trying desperately to escape.

"That's what I said," growled Harry's dad.

"We want you to come and get the little rat, that's what we want! Talk about trouble! Me and my mates, we never seen anything like it!"

Harry felt his heart give a leap, just as a big grin started to spread across his father's face. Kim took her arm away and clasped her hands together with glee.

"So she's safe?" asked Dad.

"Yeah, the dog's OK. But it nearly took my bleedin' finger off."

"Where did you find her?"

"Running in the road – could've got squashed by a bus! Anyway, there was five of us, and we sorta surrounded it, but it wasn't easy to catch, no way! Might be small, this thing, but it puts up a fight.

50

Never stops yapping, neither. Give us a
headache if you don't get here quick!"

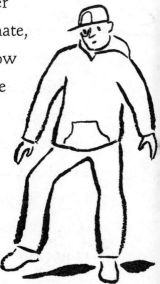

"That's my Bonnie," whispered
Harry. He wanted to burst into tears
– of happiness this time – but
stopped himself.

"Anyway, you better
come and fetch her, mate,
cos we're in the flat now
and we don't want to be
seen out with her, know
what I mean? Bit of a
girl's dog, innit?"

Harry wanted to grab
the phone and yell "NO,
SHE ISN'T!" – but then
he remembered he'd

said the same thing
when Mum had first brought
Bonnie home. How wrong can
you be? he thought.

In a daze he saw his dad scribbling instructions on a piece of paper before saying thank you about five times and putting down the phone.

The three of them stared at one another, smiling happily.

"How lucky are you, Harry?" Dad said quietly, shaking his head. "And how *lucky* is that dog?"

They were out of the door in minutes, following the route Bonnie must have taken. Harry rang his mum on his mobile to tell her that Bonnie was safe, but he didn't mention the number of busy roads she must have crossed as she made her great escape.

At last they found themselves
towered over by blocks of flats,
standing next to a wire fence
which seemed to run all around
the housing estate.

Harry felt scared again. "Where
did he tell us to go?" he whispered.

"The guy said to wait in the
middle over there, by that tree."

They went to stand by the
single tree which had battled
its way out of the earth in
that windswept place. All the
windows of the flats gazed
down on them blankly.
There was nobody
to be seen.

Suddenly Kim
gripped Harry's arm.

"Look over there!" she whispered.

A metal door clanged open. Harry saw
four tall men striding towards them with an
odd rolling walk, as if they were on a boat
at sea. His heart started to beat very fast.
Was that...?

Yes! One of them was carrying something
which squiggled and wriggled in his arms –

54

a squirming flurry
of white, as if a
snowball had come
to life.

"Bonnie!" yelled Harry.
The man carrying her
just had time to bend down
and put her on the ground
before Bonnie leaped free.
Now the snowball was jet-
propelled, driven along by the
force of its waving white flag of a tail.
It tore across the open space until Harry
scooped it up.

"Hello, Mouse-Face! Hello, girl!" he
spluttered, giggling with happiness as
Bonnie licked his face all over.

The gang of men reached them. Close up
they were younger than Harry had thought,
all about twenty, all with shaven heads and
hooded tops. The one who'd been carrying

Bonnie had the words **LOVE** and **HATE** tattooed across his knuckles, and another had a tattoo of a skull on his neck just below his right ear. The third had a pierced eyebrow, and the fourth wore a baseball cap pulled low over a rather painful-looking black eye.

"All right?" said **LOVE** and **HATE**, nodding at Harry's dad.

"Yeah. I'm Dave, and this is Kim and—"

"Thanks for finding Bonnie!" blurted out Harry, holding her close.

"I'm Dan," said **LOVE** and **HATE**, who seemed to be the leader. "That's Baz, an' Pete, an' Smiffy."

They all nodded coolly.

"I'm Haz!" said Harry.

"Can you tell us what happened?" asked Kim.

Dan told them how they'd been walking along when they saw the little dog scurrying about in the road by some parked cars. "We knew it wasn't no stray," he said, "cos she looked too well cared for, know what I mean? So we tried to catch her – we thought she might get hurt. But she wasn't easy to get hold of, was she, lads?" He looked at his friends, who shook their heads.

"Put up a real fight!" said Smiffy, the one with the baseball cap.

"Proper little scrapper!" said Pete, the one with the pierced eyebrow.

"One mean mutt!" said Baz, the one with the skull tattoo.

"Still got the tooth marks!" said Dan, waggling his finger.

Harry laughed out loud – and they all
joined in. He put Bonnie down, and she ran
round in circles at their feet,
yapping like mad when Dan
tried to pick her up.

He grinned. "See
what I mean?"

"You went to a lot
of trouble," said
Harry's dad.

"Nah," said Dan,
shuffling his feet and
looking embarrassed.
"We like dogs, don't
we, lads? Not that this is
a *proper* dog, know what
I mean?"

For once, Harry didn't mind people teasing Bonnie. Yes, she was tiny, but she'd walked around London all by herself, crossed busy roads, stood up to this gang of strangers, and been taken prisoner only after a fight!

"She may be a toy dog, but she's the bravest toy dog in England," said Kim.

"Respect," said Dan.

The four men started to walk away, but Harry's dad called after them. "Look, guys," he said, "I'm really … I mean, you haven't asked… Hey, take this and buy yourselves a beer on us, OK?"

He pulled out his wallet and offered them a twenty pound note, which Dan took with a big grin.

"Don't mind if we do, mate – thanks!"

Baz gave Harry a friendly pat on the head. "And listen, son, you better keep her locked up safe. People could steal a dog like that."

"Yeah, loads of dodgy blokes round here," grinned Dan – and they all roared with laughter, sticking their thumbs up to say goodbye as they walked away.

For a while Harry, Dad and Kim walked towards home in silence. Harry had brought Bonnie's lead, and she pulled ahead, sniffing at walls and gates, just as she always did. Each of them was imagining what could have happened to Bonnie. Harry was imagining a kidnapper demanding a briefcase full of money; Kim was imagining a woman stealing Bonnie just because she was such a cute lapdog; Dad was imagining the little dog getting run over – he'd never have been able to face Harry or his Mum again.

But it was all right.

At last Harry said, "They were really good guys, Dad."

"They certainly didn't *look* it!" said Kim.

"Just goes to show…" said Dad thoughtfully.

"Funny, isn't it?" said Harry. "I mean, you see people like them walking along and you feel, you know, a bit scared. But they took *care* of Bonnie! Aren't we lucky?"

"That's for sure," said his dad, letting out a whoosh of breath.

Later, when they were back at the flat, Dad suddenly said, "I hope… I mean… This hasn't put you off coming to stay with me and Kim again, has it, big guy?"

"It wasn't *your* fault, Dad," Harry replied. "Anyway, this has been the best ever proof about Bonnie – I can't wait to tell Zena and Zack and Susie! I mean, those four men, they looked bad but they weren't; and Bonnie doesn't look big but she *is*!"

"Definitely. Give her a hoodie and an earring and she'd be leader of the pack," laughed Dad.

"Don't forget the tattoo!" giggled Kim. "What would it say?"

"Brave Dog Bonnie!" yelled Harry.

And Bonnie growled, "Grrrrr – rrrrrr … *grrrrr*!" to prove him right.

BONNIE was still struggling when they reached the block of flats. She didn't like this place, and the smelly lift was *terrifying*. But she couldn't show how scared she was. So she set up a long, low growl deep in her throat, to frighten away the fear.

Bang! went the door behind them, and only then did they put her down on the floor. Bonnie squared up to her captors: hind legs out, chest forward, barking at them with all the power in her lungs. She ran from room to room, but the flat was small and there was nowhere to hide.

I'll deafen them, she thought. I'll cause such trouble, I'll make them sorry! And I'll start by chewing their trousers, she decided, making a run at the nearest pair of jeans and grabbing on with all the strength she could muster.

"Blimey, here we go again!" said the man. But he didn't sound very scared.

* Iron Dog *

Harry felt Bonnie's familiar shape through
the duvet and listened to the unfamiliar
sounds of London outside. His dad and Kim
were still asleep. He thought of yesterday
and wanted to pull Bonnie right in under the
bedclothes, to keep her safe.

"Still, it's not so bad here, is it, Bons?" he
whispered. "And we've got a big day out
today."

Dad had told them that on his very first
trip to London as a boy, he'd gone to see

one of the most famous sights in the whole world. So today they were going to visit the Tower of London.

"How exciting is that, Mouse-Face? It's where all the kings and queens stayed, and some of them had their heads chopped off! It's a really old place, and they've got suits of armour and swords and the Crown jewels – and everything!"

Bonnie rolled over on her back and stuck all four paws in the air, wanting her pink tummy to be rubbed. Laughing, Harry obeyed. "OK, OK, it's not so interesting to you, is it?"

After breakfast they all set out. Kim looked very cool in her black leather jacket, and before he could stop himself Harry told her he liked it. Her cheeks went pink, and Dad's grin split his face from ear to ear. "Isn't she gorgeous?" he said proudly, giving her a hug.

Immediately a part of Harry wished he had kept quiet. Mum's just as pretty, protested a small voice inside his head.

Then it was time for the dreaded Underground again, which Bonnie hated. To tell the truth, Harry wasn't so keen on it either. There was something horrible about being hurtled through dark tunnels far beneath the city streets. Dad told him that this train line went round and round the same track all day, which was why it was called the Circle Line. Harry wondered if the drivers ever got dizzy. Secretly he was missing Mum, and the Tube just made that feeling worse. It was the strangeness of it all; it was all so far from their old life…

He wished Bonnie would stop shivering, but he did enjoy the way everybody stared at her and said, "Aaaah, look!"

"You can't take Bonnie anywhere without her getting a fan club!" smiled Kim.

It seemed a
very long way on
the train, heading
east to Tower Hill, but
when they left the station
the sun was shining.

"Look!" yelled Harry in excitement – for
there was the River Thames glittering in the
bright morning light.

Bonnie danced around on the end of her
lead. Dad pointed out the boats chugging
to and fro, and explained how the famous
Tower Bridge would lift in the middle to
let any big ships through. Crowds of
tourists wandered past the
long wall that

surrounded the Tower of London itself. Stalls sold souvenirs.

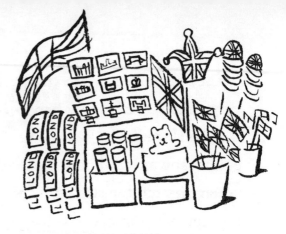

Everything seemed to buzz. Harry wanted to leap about just like Bonnie; for the first time on his visit to London he felt the thrill of being where so much was happening.

But when they reached the ticket office his mood changed. Only guide dogs were allowed in.

"I can't believe I didn't think of that," groaned his dad.

"What shall we do?" wailed Harry.

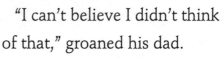

Except Guide Dogs

They all looked at one another helplessly.

Then Kim clapped her hands together.
"I know!" she said. "I've been to the Tower
before; and anyway, this should be special
father–son time, shouldn't it? So Bonnie and
I will go for a stroll across the bridge and
along the river. It's a gorgeous day and I feel
like some exercise. I'll pick up sandwiches,
and when you've finished we'll find a bench
and have a picnic!"

There was no arguing. Kim held out her
hand for the lead, and even though
Bonnie didn't want to leave Harry,
she had no choice.

"Keep in touch!" Kim
called back to them,
waving her mobile
in the air.

Secretly Harry was glad. It was great to walk along beside Dad, with nobody else to interrupt them – not even Bonnie. It'd been a long time since Harry had felt so happy and free from worries. Dad had always loved history and was telling him lots of stories about the Tower of London; but to tell the truth, Harry was hardly listening. It was just too exciting to be *there*.

"Why are those men in funny costumes, Dad?" he asked.

"They're the famous Beefeaters, son. Hundreds of years ago, they were the royal bodyguard, but these days they're old soldiers who've had long careers in the military. The tourists love them; there's nothing more English than a Beefeater..."

"So do they eat steak all the time?" asked Harry, and Dad laughed.

They walked along the ramparts, with the river on their right. Harry looked up at the flag fluttering off the central White Tower and whispered, "This is *awesome*!"

And it was. Dad told him about
Traitors' Gate, where centuries ago grand
people condemned to prison – and even
death – would arrive by boat. They saw the
Bloody Tower, where two little princes were
said to have been murdered by their own
uncle long ago. Harry shivered and was glad
to step back out into the sunlight, where
they watched the Tower's famous ravens,

 which were supposed to bring good
luck to the whole of
England. Dad was
so full of stories!
It was brilliant.

Inside the main part of the castle, called the White Tower, Harry wandered among rows of suits of armour and imagined what it would feel like to sit on a horse weighed down with all that metal. They examined spears and lances and daggers and very old guns, and talked about how brave men must have been to go into battle in those days.

The Crown jewels were next. Harry and Dad stood on a moving walkway which carried them

past crowns and coronets, all twinkling with rubies, emeralds, diamonds and pearls, safe in their glass cases.

"Shall we snatch one to take home for Mum?" whispered Dad.

"She's already bought Bonnie a collar with diamonds on it," said Harry.

"No wonder you left that at home, eh?" Dad grinned.

It was when they came out at last, and Dad was just saying they ought to ring Kim, that Harry got the best surprise of the whole day. He'd already seen a lot of cannon scattered about the Tower grounds, but for the first time he noticed the one in front of the White Tower. They'd walked past it once before, but now...

"Dad, look!" he exclaimed. "It's a dog!"

They went nearer.

Sure enough, the barrel of the cannon was supported by the unmistakable shape of a dog: a white dog with floppy ears.

"It's ... it's a Bonnie dog!" Harry yelled.
"A ginormous Maltese!"

"Wow!" said Dad.

"Awesome!" said Harry.

Dad read from the information board. This amazing cannon decorated with green snakes and hands clutching daggers had been paid for by some soldiers called the Knights of Malta, and that was why the part underneath had been cast in the shape of a Maltese dog.

"The gun bit is made of bronze and the bottom is iron. It's called a twenty-four pounder – and it's about four hundred years old! Look at the lions' heads poking from the centre of the wheels, Harry."

But Harry wasn't interested in the lions. "It's made Bonnie into a giant!" he laughed. "A great big iron dog!"

"A great big *brave* iron dog," said Dad, "going to war and everything! I bet this Maltese saw some battles!"

"Bonnie was an iron dog yesterday, wasn't she, Dad?"

"That's for sure!"

Harry dug out his mobile phone and took
lots of pictures of the Maltese cannon to
show his mum, while Dad rang Kim and
arranged a meeting place. Then there was
just time to visit the Tower of London shop.
There were no postcards of the Maltese
cannon, but Harry spent
some of the pocket
money Dad had
given him on a teddy
bear dressed like a
Beefeater for Mum.

And Dad bought him a pen and pencil set, a notebook, a rubber and a mug – all showing the Tower of London.

When they met up with Kim and Bonnie, the little dog went mad, jumping off the ground with all four paws, until Harry picked her up. "Oh, am I glad to see you, Iron Dog!" he said as she covered his face with licks.

"How was it?" Dad asked Kim.

"Not easy at first," she admitted. "This dog's got her own ideas about where she goes! She dug her paws in and kept looking back at the Tower, because she knew you were there, Harry. She came along in the end, but she's a stubborn little thing."

"Iron Dog!" repeated Harry with a laugh.

Kim looked puzzled until she heard about the Maltese dog cannon and Harry showed her the pictures on his phone. Then they strolled to a bench looking across the river and ate their picnic.

Harry felt happy, and strong somehow. Now he'd come face to face with the iron dog, he felt that nothing could ever scare him again.

The next day, Dad picked up his car from the garage and they set off home. Harry had been terrified Kim would want to come, but she had lots of work to do so she stayed behind in London.

She bent to give Harry a quick peck on his cheek and said she hoped he'd come and visit them again soon. "We could go and see a show," she suggested.

"I'd better leave Bonnie with Mum then," he said. "Who knows what she might get up to next time!" But really he was thinking that it would be different next time anyway. He wouldn't need the support of his little iron dog.

Half an hour from home Harry called Mum as she'd asked, and when they arrived there was a surprise party to greet him and Bonnie. Zena, Zack and Susie had put a balloon on the door with **WELCOME HOME**

written on it in marker pen, and
Princess Daisy the (annoying) chihuahua
was running round in circles, yapping at
Bonnie as if *she* owned their home! Bonnie
had to make a couple of fierce runs at her
to put her back in her place.

At first Harry didn't really want to hug Mum in front of everybody, but Bonnie solved that one. She jumped around Mum's ankles in mad excitement, begging to be picked up, so then it was natural for Mum to hold out her other arm and call, "Group hug, eh, Harry?"

"That's what I like about that dog," said Dad. "She's not afraid to show how she feels."

Mum loved her Beefeater teddy, and Harry showed his friends his Tower of London souvenirs. Then they all helped themselves

to cakes and biscuits as he told everybody the story of Bonnie's great adventure with the scary-looking men.

"But they were OK," said Dad, shaking his head in disbelief.

"They were more than OK," protested Harry. "They were cool – and they really loved Bonnie, although they pretended not to."

Mum shuddered. "To think what might have happened to her."

"No, *don't* think about it," piped up Zena helpfully.

"Anyway, then we met a statue of Bonnie showing what she's really like inside," said Dad. "Go on, show them your pics, Harry."

And so Harry told them all about the iron dog of Malta, who had been guarding the Tower of London for four hundred years. Mum laughed as she looked over to where their pet was terrorizing Princess Daisy in the corner.

"We're lucky we've got her to guard *us* for ever, aren't we, Harry?" And she smiled.

BONNIE wasn't pleased — not at all. First there was the horrible noisy train again, and then Harry was walking away and she couldn't follow. She looked up at the woman who was holding the lead and yapped. Bonnie didn't want to go with her; she wanted to stay right there and wait for Harry. So she sat down and wouldn't budge.

The woman started tugging. "Oh, please come with me, Bonnie," she begged. "Be nice to me, because if you are, Harry will be too — in the end. *Please* help make Harry like me, Bonnie."

Bonnie looked up again. She liked the woman's voice ... but no, she wanted to stay.

Then suddenly she spotted a brown and white dog in the distance prancing along on the end of a lead. What dog was it? What would its scent be like? The curiosity was too much for Bonnie, so she got up and trotted towards it.

That was just where the woman wanted to go,
and Bonnie heard her cry, "Good girl!
Thank you, Bonnie!"
Humans are sweet really, Bonnie thought.
They always think you're doing what they want,
when actually you're just doing what *you*
want — all the time.
Anyway, Harry was back in a couple of tail
wags, and now they were all home together again.
Everything smelled the same; Harry's mum's
cuddles felt the same.
Yes, this is my territory, thought Bonnie happily;
this is where I belong. But that annoying chihuahua
doesn't! Oh well, back to business. Grrrrr...
I'll soon remind her who
the big dog is!

BRAVE DOG BONNIE – A TRUE STORY

By Bel Mooney

Children often ask me if my stories are "real". Perhaps they know that my own little Maltese is called Bonnie, and came from the rescue home, just like Harry's Bonnie.

Perhaps they know, too, that I once wrote many, many stories inspired by my own daughter, Kitty. So when I go to school and book events to meet my readers, I tell them that writers can get their ideas from anywhere. And everywhere.

But the most exciting event in this book *did* happen! I took Bonnie to London on the train, but because I had to go and see some important journalists, a friend met me to look after her for most of the day. But Bonnie didn't like that, and so she squeezed under a gate and ran off – probably in search of me. When my friend realized, he was so upset. He looked for her for ages. He was nearly in tears when he couldn't find her.

Then came the phone call ... because of course, all dogs should wear a collar with a phone number on it. And yes, the real Bonnie had been picked up by some very scary-looking young men, just like the Bonnie in this book. Can you imagine how I felt? But they were so kind to her – and, like Harry and his dad, I realized that you can't always tell what a person is like from the way he or she looks.

Oh, but was I glad to get my Bonnie back!

MISSING

Small white dog with big personality

Small Dog, Big World!

Bonnie and Harry have fun in London.
Can you match the tourist attraction to the
city (and country) in which it is found?

Eiffel Tower

Colosseum

Taj Mahal

Central Park

Burj Khalifa

Dubai (Saudi Arabia)

Agra (India)

Rome (Italy)

Paris (France)

New York (USA)

Love Bonnie? Then why not read all six of her tail-wagging adventures!

To find out more about the books and the real-life Bonnie who inspired them, visit belmooney.co.uk

Bel Mooney is a well-known journalist
and author of many books for adults and
children, including the hugely popular Kitty series.
She lives in Bath with her husband and real-life
Maltese dog, Bonnie, who is the inspiration
for this series. Bel says of the real Bonnie:
"She makes me laugh and transforms my life
with her intelligence, courage and affection.
And I just know she's going to pick out a really
good card for my birthday."

Find out more about Bel at belmooney.co.uk

Sarah McMenemy is a highly respected artist
who illustrates for magazines and newspapers
and has worked on diverse commissions all
over the world, including art for the London
Underground, CD covers and stationery. She
illustrated the bestselling City Skylines series and
is the creator of the picture books *Waggle*
and *Jack's New Boat*. She lives in London.

Find out more about Sarah at
sarahmcmenemy.com